minions™

BIG BOSS STICKER BOOK

OR

CAN YOU FIND A BANANA OR THE VILLAIN-CON LOGO HIDDEN ON EVERY PAGE?

D0752120

LITTLE, BROWN & COMPANY
LB kids

Minions © 2015 Universal Studios. Minions is a trademark and copyright of Universal Studios. Licensed by Universal Studios Licensing LLC. All rights reserved.
2015 © Universal Studios Licensing LLC

In accordance with the U.S. Copyright Act of 1976, the scanning, uploading, and electronic sharing of any part of this book without the permission of the publisher is unlawful piracy and theft of the author's intellectual property. If you would like to use material from the book (other than for review purposes), prior written permission must be obtained by contacting the publisher at permissions@hbgusa.com. Thank you for your support of the author's rights.

Little, Brown and Company

Hachette Book Group
1290 Avenue of the Americas, New York, NY 10104
Visit us at lb-kids.com

LB kids is an imprint of Little, Brown and Company.
The LB kids name and logo are trademarks of Hachette Book Group, Inc.

The publisher is not responsible for websites (or their content) that are not owned by the publisher.

First Edition: November 2015
Content previously published in *Minions Activity Book* and *Minions Sticker Book* in 2015 by Centum.

ISBN 978-0-316-30001-8

10 9 8 7 6 5 4 3 2 1

APS

PRINTED IN CHINA

minionsmovie.com

ALL ABOUT . . . KEVIN

He's the Minion with a plan . . . to save his buddies from a boring life without a master.

ALIASES:
Kevin, Kev-bo, Seventh Kevin, Sir Kevin

CHARACTER TRAITS:
Proud, "big brother," not so great at public speaking

GADGETS USED:
Lava-Lamp Gun and Herb's ultimate weapon

DISLIKES:
Disappointing his big boss

KEY MOMENTS:

The discovery of the Minions' iconic blue overalls

Playing polo while riding a corgi

Ultimately leading the Minions to their perfect master

[Add your favorite Kevin moment here]

_____

_____

LIKES:
Protecting his buddies, spending time with Stuart and Bob, Lava-Lamp Guns, epic adventures, flying in Scarlet's jet, heists, Villain-Con, police chases, the Nelson family

The Minions need some business cards to give out at Villain-Con if they're going to find a new master.

Design one for them below!

ALL ABOUT...
STUART

He's the musical Minion who loves nothing more than getting up onstage and playing his ukulele.

LIKES:
Playing his ukulele, hot tubs

ALIASES:
Stuart, Stu, Stu-art, Stu-perman, Beef Stu

CHARACTER TRAITS:
Cool, musical, flirt, hungry

GADGETS USED:
Hypno-Hat

DISLIKES:
Snow globes

KEY MOMENTS:

Falling in love with a yellow fire hydrant

Relaxing in the hot tub in his thong bikini

Rocking out in front of Buckingham Palace

[Add your favorite Stuart moment here]

_____

_____

_____

Stuart has lost his precious ukulele. Can you help him find it? It's the one that's different from all the rest.

HOW DID YOU DO? Check your answer on page 62.

ALL ABOUT . . .
BOB

The littlest Minion, who is excited about everything—especially his teddy, Tim. What he lacks in size, he makes up for in heart.

LIKES:
His teddy bear, Tim; giggling; playing hide-and-seek; making friends

ALIASES:
Bob, Robert, Bobby, My boy, King Bob

CHARACTER TRAITS:
Overly excitable, sweet, loyal, lovable, "little brother"

GADGETS USED:
Stretch Suit

KEY MOMENTS:

Making Tim dance when asked for special skills at evil henchmen placement stand

Swallowing the red ruby

Pulling the sword from the stone

[Add your favorite Bob moment here]

DISLIKES:
Bees, being away from his buddies, losing Tim

How many Tims can you count below? _____

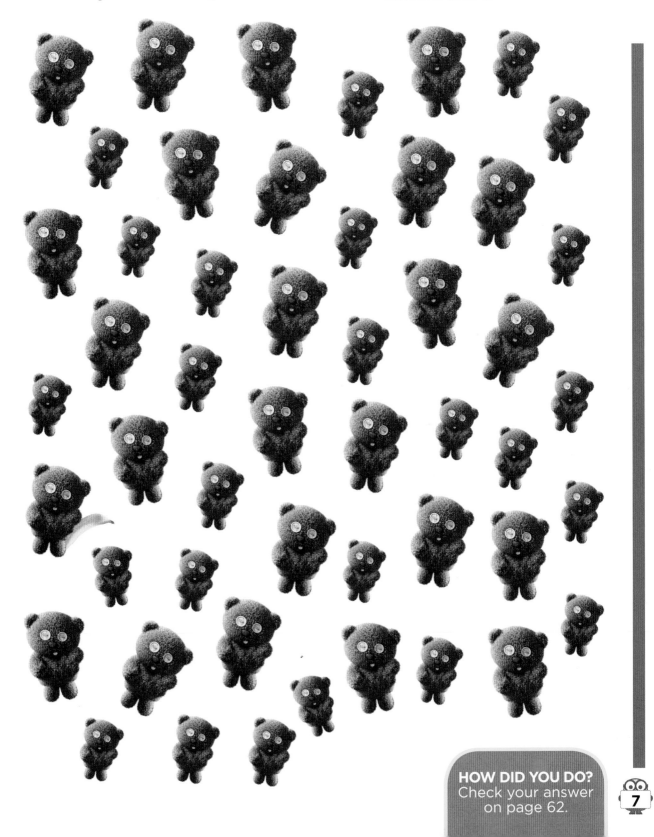

HOW DID YOU DO?
Check your answer
on page 62.

7

MASTERS THROUGH HISTORY:
T. REX

**Minions only have one aim in life—
to serve the most despicable master around.**

And after following evil amoebae, fish, and amphibians
for millennia, the next big step was, of course, T. rex!

MASTER PROS:

- T. rex was mean
- Great ROAR
- Also doubles as mode
  of transportation

MASTER FAIL:

- T. rex was vulnerable to
  death when he fell into
  a volcano!

DID YOU KNOW?
- T. rex's name means **tyrant lizard**.
- T. rex lived 70 million years ago.
- T. rex was 40 feet long. That's about
  the same length as a bus!

MINION: COPY AND DRAW

Can you copy this picture of a Minion in the grid below?

DON'T FORGET TO ADD SOME YELLOW—AND OTHER COLORS!

DINO: COLORING

As a master, the T. rex was not only evil but also so large he could carry around lots of Minions on his back while they polished his scales. Roarsome! Color in the scene below.

ADD SOME MORE MINIONS TO THE T. REX SO THEY CAN PAMPER THEIR MASTER!

WORD-SEARCHASAURUS

The Minions are spending a lot of time searching for the most despicable master they can find. Can you find all these roarific words below?

PREHISTORIC   VOLCANO
DINOSAUR   BIG BOSS
MINIONS   TEETH
T. REX   CLAW

How many times can you find the word *ROAR* in the grid? _____

```
J X X H L X P O I U Y T E R E
D V S J K A D X P I U Y X R Q
R O A R J G F S N O I N I M Q
R L X V M U Y R Y U R D F G A
X C C B N F R O T R O R E S S
P A V C U S O A X K A F G H D
O N B X F G A R O A R A O R F
I O N T L H R X J X R O D U X
U X D E D F G H H Q C S X A G
Y P R E H I S T O R I C J S H
T X O T L H S R H O L R A O R
R F A H K X F E J A E R O N R
E D R B J B L X W R R T Y I J
H D X V C V I P P H G R T D K
G S X S S O B G I B X X X X L
```

HOW DID YOU DO? Check your answers on page 62.

BANANA PUZZLE

Using your stickers, can you finish the puzzle to find out what the Minions are so excited to find beneath the rock?

UH-OH! ONE OF THE JIGSAW PIECES IS FLIPPED. CAN YOU DRAW THE MISSING PART OF THE PICTURE INSTEAD?

HOW DID YOU DO?
Check your answer on page 62.

DINO DOODLE DISASTER

It started with a banana (doesn't everything!), but somehow the Minions ended up with their T. rex master falling into a volcano. How did this accident occur?

Doodle the action in the blank boxes below.

USE YOUR STICKERS TO DECORATE THE SCENES, TOO!

MASTERS THROUGH HISTORY: CAVEMAN

When Minions met man, they knew they were on to a good thing.

Although man was shorter and hairier than T. rex, he was much smarter. Unfortunately, early man was apparently quite delicious.

MASTER PROS:

- Stylish use of fur clothing!
- Fun tools
- Complimentary cave

MASTER FAIL:

- Bears think cavemen are very tasty!

DID YOU KNOW?
- We and early humans are all part of the same family called *Homo sapiens*.
- *Homo sapien* means **knowing man**.

SQUIGGLY LINE OF DESTINY

Minions may all look the same, but they're actually quite unique.

For example, these three Minions are all in search of something different.

Follow the paths and find out what each one is looking for—and who will be surprised by a bear!

HOW DID YOU DO?
Check your answers on page 62.

MASTERS THROUGH HISTORY:
PHARAOH

The tribe's search for a despicable master continued through the ages, until they came to the Egyptians. Here was a society obsessed with worshipping their masters—perfect!

MASTER PROS:
- Lives in warm climate
- Fun and challenging building projects
- Cool outfits

MASTER FAIL:
- Pharaohs are easily squished by Minion-made monuments!

DID YOU KNOW?
- Pharaoh was the name given to a king or queen of ancient Egypt.
- Most ancient Egyptian pyramids were built as tombs for pharaohs.
- Both Egyptian men and women wore makeup.

HIEROGLYPHIC HIJINKS

Who's been drawing on the walls again? Oh wait, that's a Minion hieroglyphic pattern.

Can you complete each row? Use your stickers to add the next Minion in the sequences.

1

2

3

4

DECODING HIEROGLYPHICS

Reading hieroglyphics is tricky because it uses pictures instead of letters! Can you help the Minions decode a message from their master?

_ _ _ _ _   _ _   _ _   _ _ _ _ _ _ _ _ _ _ !   _ _ _

_ _ _ _ _   _ _ _ _ _ _ _   _ _ _ _

_ _ _ _   _ _ _ _ _ _ _ _ !

USE THE CODE TO CREATE YOUR OWN MESSAGE!

HOW DID YOU DO? Check your answer on page 62.

18

PYRAMID PUZZLER

The only thing the Minions forgot to put in this pyramid was the bricks. Which is kind of a big deal.

HOW TO PLAY:

- To fill the pyramid with bricks, you and a friend take turns drawing a line between two side-by-side dots.

- The player who draws the line that makes a three-sided brick wins the space, marks it with his or her initials, then takes another turn.

- Once all the bricks that can be made have been completed, the player with the most bricks **WINS**!

THE MOST POPULAR SPORT IN EGYPT IS FOOTBALL!

EGYPTIAN QUIZ

It's important that Minions know as much as possible about their master. How much do you know about the ancient Egyptians?

TEST YOUR KNOWLEDGE WITH THIS QUIZ!

1 What modern household pet did the Egyptians worship?

....

2 How many sides does a pyramid have?

....

3 What shape were the stones used to build the pyramids?

....

4 What were the pyramids made from?

....

5 What was a pharaoh?

....

6 What is the name of the river that runs through Egypt?

....

7 What is the writing of the ancient Egyptians called?

....

8 Which picture shows the pyramid the correct way up?

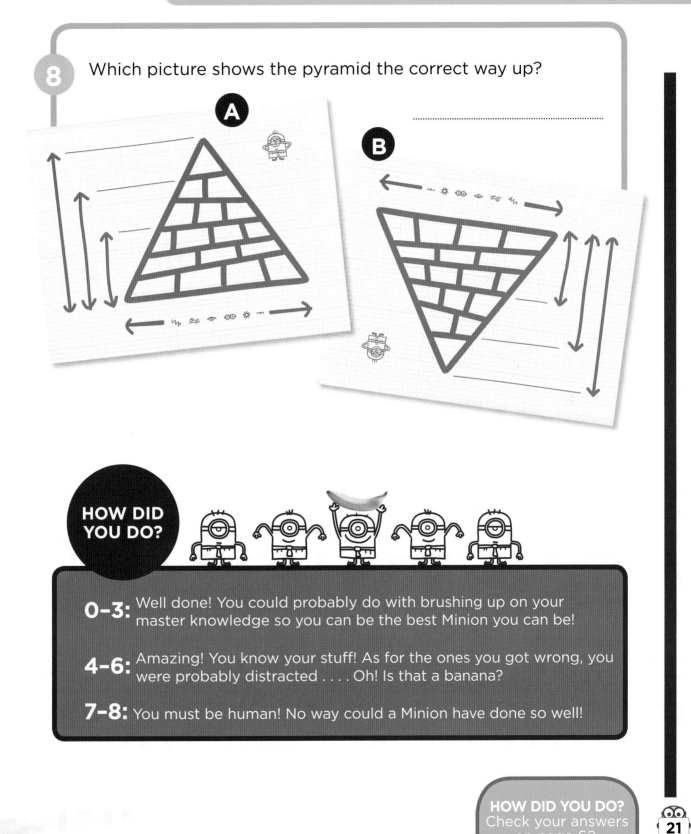

A

B

HOW DID YOU DO?

0-3: Well done! You could probably do with brushing up on your master knowledge so you can be the best Minion you can be!

4-6: Amazing! You know your stuff! As for the ones you got wrong, you were probably distracted . . . . Oh! Is that a banana?

7-8: You must be human! No way could a Minion have done so well!

HOW DID YOU DO?
Check your answers on page 62.

BUILDING SITE MAZE

START →

Can you help the Minions get the stones through the maze to the building site?

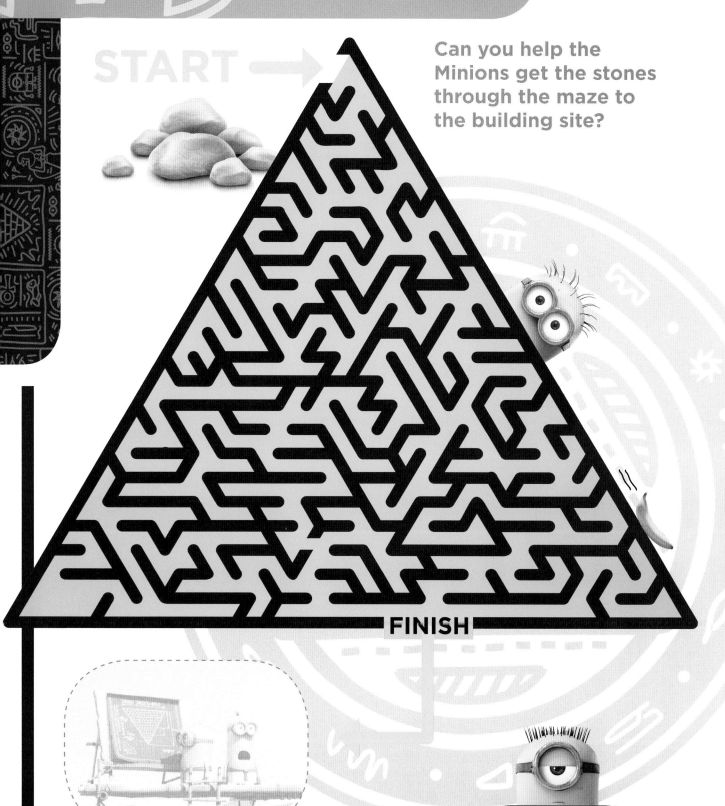

FINISH

HOW DID YOU DO?
Check your answers on page 62.

PYRAMIDS, PYRAMIDS EVERYWHERE!

Each side of a pyramid is a triangle. How many triangles can you count below?

DID YOU KNOW? OVER 130 PYRAMIDS HAVE BEEN DISCOVERED IN EGYPT.

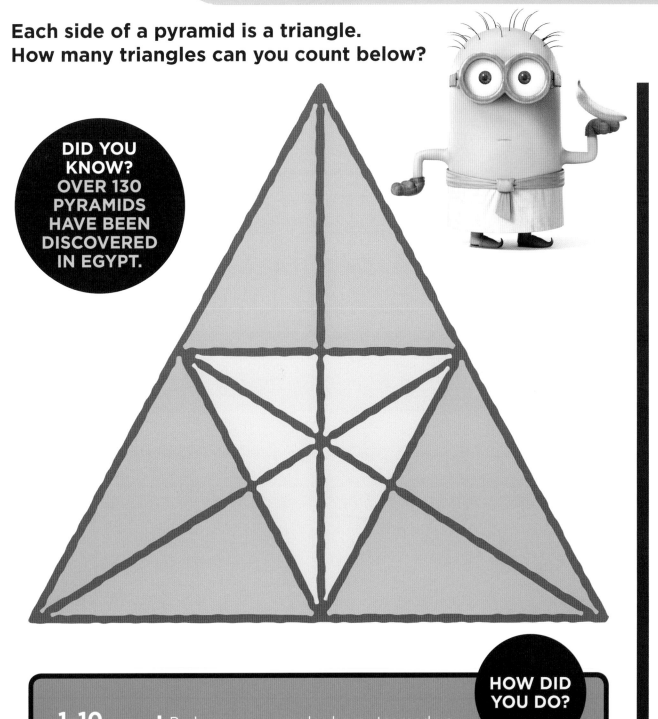

HOW DID YOU DO?

1–10 : Perhaps your goggles have steamed up— clean them and try counting again.

11–20 : Impressive! Who needs more than twenty triangles anyway when there are so many other shapes to build!

Over 20 : WOW! Have a banana to celebrate!

MASTERS THROUGH HISTORY:
DRACULA

The Minions loved working for Dracula.

He partied all night and slept all day.
The Minions knew Dracula loved parties
so much that they decided to throw him
a special bash for his 357th birthday.

MASTER PROS:

- Mean AND spooky
- Sweet cape
- No cooking required

MASTER FAIL:

- Dracula turns to dust
  when exposed to
  sunlight—oops!

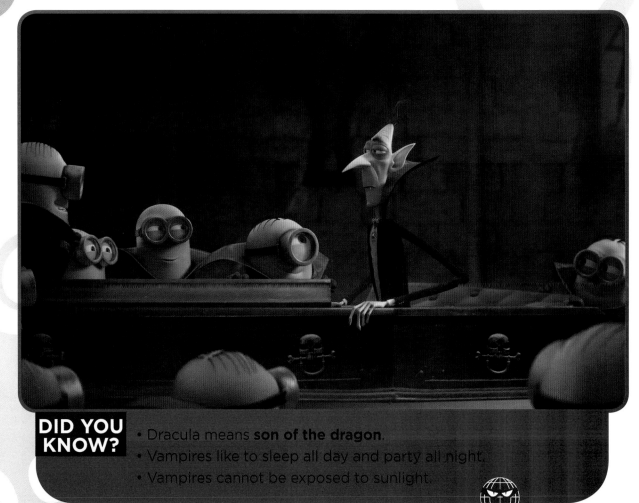

DID YOU KNOW?

- Dracula means **son of the dragon**.
- Vampires like to sleep all day and party all night.
- Vampires cannot be exposed to sunlight.

BIRTHDAY BLOOPER

Dracula's 357th birthday didn't quite go as planned!

Find the missing jigsaw piece stickers to show what went wrong and complete the picture.

WHAT A PAIN IN THE NECK!
One of the pieces is wrong. Use your pens to finish the picture instead.

HOW DID YOU DO?
Check your answer on page 62.

MASTERS THROUGH HISTORY:
Pirate

The Minions were happy to serve their pirate master.

It meant sailing, piles of plunder, great outfits, cool songs, and a language that was just as incomprehensible as their own!

But before long it was the same sad story . . . .

Master pros:
- Life at sea!
- No showers required
- Cool catchphrases

Master fail:
- Pirates are just the right size to be shark bait!

DID YOU KNOW?
- Pirates had many superstitions and believed that piercing their ears would improve their eyesight.
- Most pirating happened between 1690 and 1720.
- Pirates used compasses to navigate.

Where's the flag?

What's this?! Minion pirates without a flag?
Oh, no, no, no, NO! This will never do.

Help these Minions find their flag without getting eaten by a hungry shark. If they DO get eaten by a hungry shark, you can skip the flag part.

FINISH

START

HOW DID YOU DO?
Check your answer on page 62.

27

Ahoy! A map in a Minion!

Let's sail the seven seas!
The Minions will follow their
master anywhere. Can you help
the Minions follow their pirate
master to the treasure?

**FOLLOW THE PATTERN
THROUGH THE MAZE IN
THIS ORDER:**

START

FINISH

HOW DID YOU DO?
Check your answer
on page 63.

JOKE:
Why are pirates called pirates?
They just AARRRGGHHH!

Pirate ship doodle

Uh-oh! The Minions have been fishing and brought a hungry shark on board. Color in the picture, but beware of the jaws . . . they bite!

SEA-DOKU

Can you help complete the tricky puzzle below using your stickers?

Each number should appear only once in each box, row, and column.

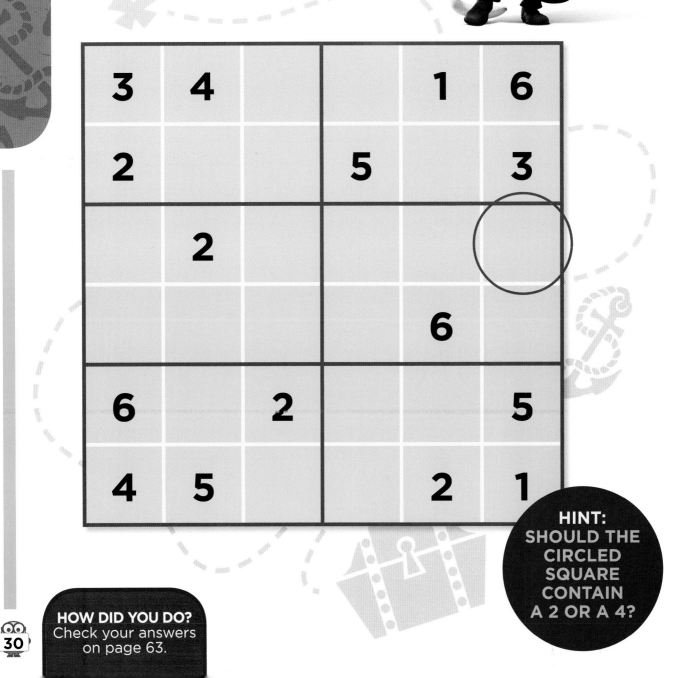

HINT:
SHOULD THE
CIRCLED
SQUARE
CONTAIN
A 2 OR A 4?

HOW DID YOU DO?
Check your answers
on page 63.

Scramble and solve!

Clear your goggles—it's time to put your mind to work. After a rough night at sea, these words have been muddled up.

TARIPES ....

EYA TEAMY ....

HIPS ....

YOHA ....

RAKSH ....

REASTURE ....

DUPLNER ....

KPLAN ....

My pirate storyboard

Can you make up a hilarious story about the Minions and their pirate master? Draw the scenes in the boxes and don't forget to add captions and use your stickers, too!

WALK THE PLANK

MASTERS THROUGH HISTORY: NAPOLEON BONAPARTE

Ah, Napoleon—short, power crazy, and fond of conquering countries.

The Minions thought they'd found their perfect master fit at last. But all too soon the dream was over, and the Minions found themselves out in the cold.

MASTER PROS:

- Leader of France
- Exciting travel opportunities
- A real emperor

MASTER FAIL:

- Napoleon (and his army) didn't appreciate "blow up the leader"!

DID YOU KNOW?
- Napoleon's nickname was **Little Commander**.
- After being exiled on an island, he escaped and took over Paris again.
- He once wrote a romance novel.

VIVE LE MINION

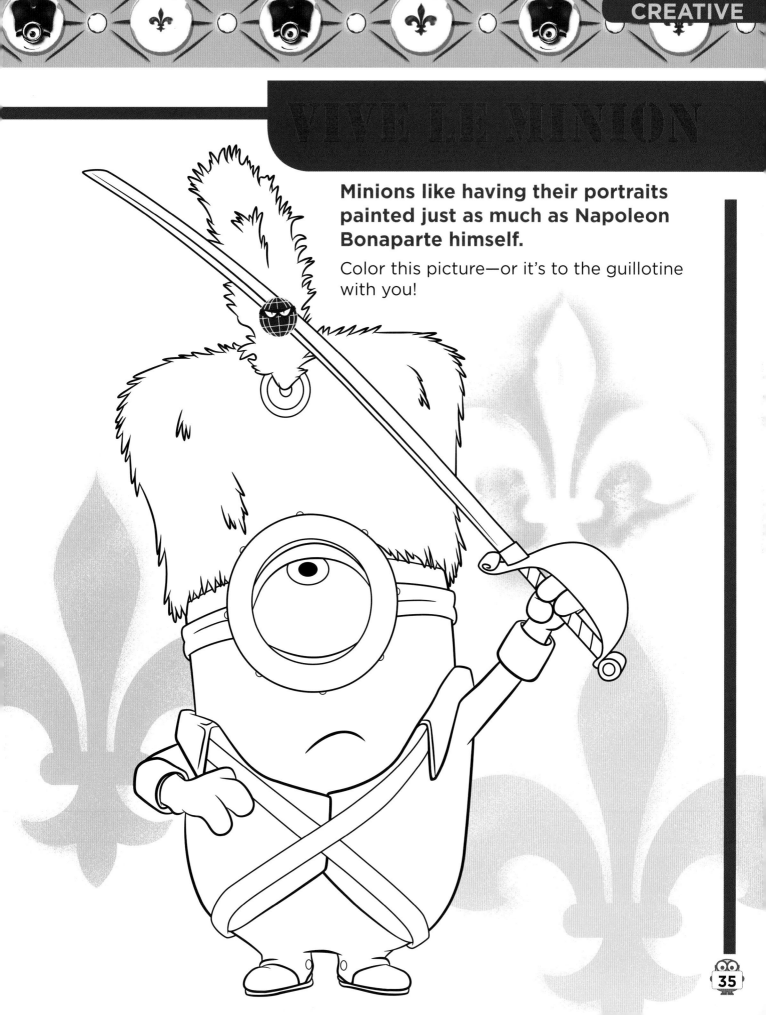

Minions like having their portraits painted just as much as Napoleon Bonaparte himself.

Color this picture—or it's to the guillotine with you!

MASTERS FROM THE PAST

How much did you learn about the Minions' past masters?

Take this true or false quiz to find out.

1
T. rex's name means "tyrant master."

True or **False**

2
T. rex lived 7 million years ago.

True or **False**

3
Cavemen made paintings on the inside of caves.

True or **False**

4
Homo sapien means "knowing man."

True or **False**

5
Ancient Egyptians called their kings or queens "pharaohs."

True or **False**

6
A pyramid is a type of tomb.

True or **False**

7 Dracula's name means "son of the bat."

True or **False**

8 Vampires cannot go out in sunlight.

True or **False**

9 Pirates pierced their ears to help eyesight.

True or **False**

10 Pirates used compasses to navigate.

True or **False**

11 Napoleon's nickname was Minion Commander.

True or **False**

12 Napoleon was the ruler of Italy.

True or **False**

How hard were you studying the Minions' past masters? Check your answers to find out:

 1-4 Must try harder. You need to do better to impress your big boss!

 5-7 Okay. You're becoming more yellow before my eyes!

8-12 You're ready! You know all there is to know about masters of the past. Now help Kevin, Stuart, and Bob journey to Villain-Con and use what they've learned to seek out the ultimate master!

HOW DID YOU DO? Check your answers on page 63.

GOING OUR WAY?

Kevin, Stuart, and Bob can't wait to get to Villain-Con!

Show the boys the fastest way from New York City to Orlando by following only this pattern.

You'll know you're close when you begin to hear shouts of ridiculous joy and glee from three certain Minions.

START

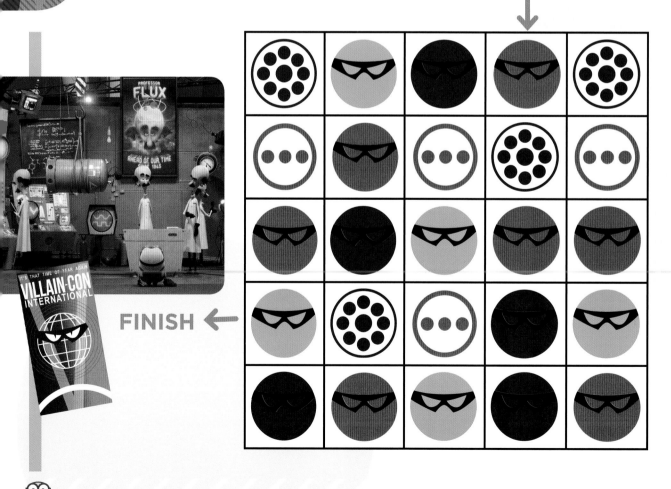

FINISH

BANANA RUN

Villain-Con can be a den of delicious distractions for any young, upcoming villain.

Help Kevin, Stuart, and Bob visit each and every bad guy booth without retracing their steps. Most importantly, make sure that the last place they visit is their favorite spot of all . . . the Banana Hut! Mmm . . . Bello!

WHICH STOP ON YOUR ROUTE IS THE SAFE CRACKING BOOTH?

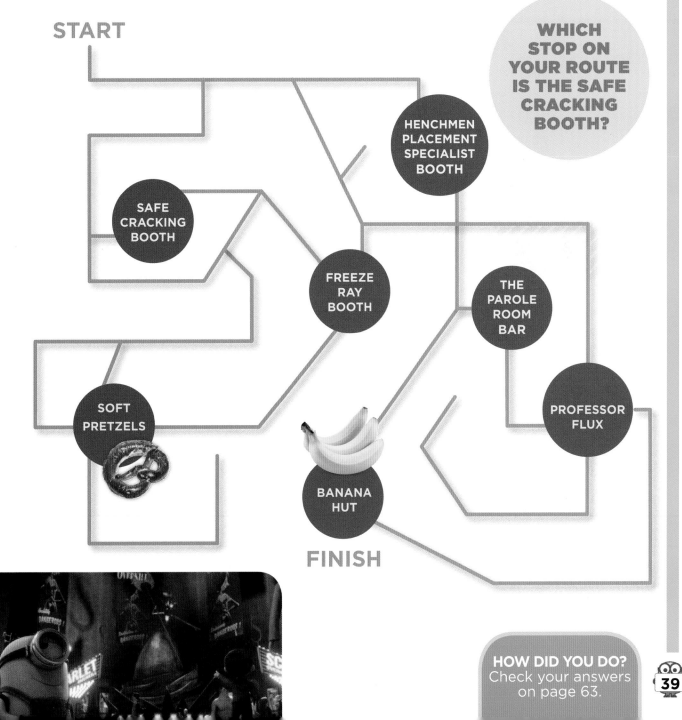

START

HENCHMEN PLACEMENT SPECIALIST BOOTH

SAFE CRACKING BOOTH

FREEZE RAY BOOTH

THE PAROLE ROOM BAR

SOFT PRETZELS

PROFESSOR FLUX

BANANA HUT

FINISH

HOW DID YOU DO?
Check your answers on page 63.

WHAT'S ON AT VILLAIN-CON?

There's so much to do at Villain-Con, so it's essential to pick up a brochure.

Read through what's happening and then try to answer the questions below.

1 If you were a villain looking for work, which booth would you visit?

2 Where would you go to learn how to freeze a bank guard for your next heist?

3 You, Kevin, Bob, and Stuart are getting hungry—where is the pretzel booth?

4 Your next caper involves getting into a safe. Where might you go to learn the skill of safe cracking?

5 Who is making a guest appearance at Villain-Con 1968?

WELCOME TO VILLAIN-CON 1968

For 89 years the biggest gathering of criminals from around the globe.

Brought to you by the Villain Network Channel— **"If you tell anyone, we'll find you!"**

545 Orange Grove Avenue **Orlando** Florida

INTERNATIONAL VILLAIN CONVENTION

DO YOU HAVE WHAT IT TAKES? FIND OUT!

Industry professionals will be on hand throughout the convention to offer critique and review your villainous skills. Ask a professional to help you on the next step of your criminal career!

Pretzels— Delicious Warm Pretzels! Even villains need to eat . . . find us next to the Parole Room Bar

There's so much to do, it's criminal:

- Attend guest lectures from esteemed villains.
- Make contacts in the underworld community.
- Learn your criminal trade.
- Sample the newest in villain technology.
- Meet your idols and even find your dream job.
- And for the first time ANYWHERE a special appearance from the first female super villain, **SCARLET OVERKILL!**

Additional Villain-Con Exclusives:

Safe Cracking Booth
Visit us and find the best way to get into that safe quickly and without fuss. It's as easy as click, click, open!

Henchmen Placement Specialist
We've been helping place the industry's best henchmen for more than 60 years. Even if you're a lizard—we'll find you that dream job!

Freeze Ray Booth
Dr. Nefario will show how to be a cool criminal with his newest gadget, the FREEZE RAY!

Sick Rick
Grab your very own copy of Sick Rick's *How to Be a Bad Guy in 10 Days.*

Villain-Con: So much fun, it's a crime!

NO PHOTOS ALLOWED.
If you would like your photograph taken with your criminal idol, please purchase one from an official Villain-Con photographer.

IT'S THAT TIME OF YEAR AGAIN

VILLAIN-CON INTERNATIONAL

LOST IN VILLAIN-CON

Ah, Villain-Con! A place where criminals can relax, see old friends, and . . . hopefully score a priceless ruby!

Kevin, Stuart, and Bob need to navigate their way to Scarlet Overkill's ruby before the other wannabe henchmen grab it.

START

FINISH

**HOW DID YOU DO?** Check your answer on page 63.

Flux's flummoxing
MEMORY GAME

Professor Flux has gotten himself in a fantastically flummoxing fiasco again! Which is the real Flux, and which is the Flux from next Thursday—who knows? It's time to test your memory.

Look at the photo below for one minute. Then turn the page and answer as many questions as you can from memory.

FLUX'S FLUMMOXING MEMORY GAME
QUESTIONS

How much do you remember from the previous page?
Let's find out!

How many
sticky notes
are on the
wall?

How many
Professor Fluxes
are there?

What time does
the clock read?

What color
are the
sticky notes?

What year
does the time
machine read?

HOW ARE
YOUR FRIENDS'
MEMORIES. TEST
EVERYONE AND
FIND OUT!

Which Minion is
standing in the
photograph?

FAR-OUT PHRASES

Have you got Herb's natural gift for cool catchphrases and wacky nicknames?

Search the grid for some of his best sayings.

GROOVY	BOBBY	MY BOY
BEEF STU	"I DIG THAT!"	
SEVENTH KEVIN	"WHO INVITED THE SQUARE?"	
KEV-BO	"THAT'S A GROOVY IDEA!"	
STU-PERMAN	"THE COOLEST!"	

HOW MANY TIMES CAN YOU FIND THE WORDS "FAR OUT" IN THE GRID?

W	H	O	I	N	V	I	T	E	D	T	H	E	S	Q	U	A	R	E	I
R	Y	V	A	N	J	N	J	A	J	S	F	Z	E	B	F	F	G	E	B
S	T	C	Y	H	S	S	T	U	P	E	R	M	A	N	A	T	L	X	Z
E	S	B	J	J	C	Q	T	V	G	A	D	G	E	T	R	U	N	R	D
R	E	M	Z	Z	W	A	O	L	B	T	V	L	W	F	O	O	P	A	K
D	L	S	T	V	B	P	B	G	A	D	G	E	T	H	U	R	D	E	C
T	O	L	T	L	E	D	L	M	T	H	L	R	M	H	T	A	Q	D	A
E	O	G	T	R	F	D	L	A	X	J	Y	X	A	L	O	F	H	I	P
K	C	A	O	P	E	V	I	U	X	F	H	F	A	R	O	U	T	Y	K
S	E	V	E	N	T	H	K	E	V	I	N	T	N	V	A	W	F	V	C
O	H	X	H	I	S	T	C	N	O	U	D	Q	A	O	E	E	L	O	A
B	T	D	Z	F	E	U	O	H	Q	I	T	A	G	K	H	O	I	O	I
E	D	W	E	N	G	O	B	G	R	O	O	V	Y	U	I	A	K	R	D
E	G	V	T	U	C	R	V	L	F	U	G	W	G	P	N	V	T	G	I
F	E	L	V	G	V	A	E	Q	J	O	I	I	G	D	M	F	H	A	G
S	T	V	L	A	A	F	K	Q	X	L	A	T	L	R	A	P	T	S	T
T	Y	A	I	V	D	I	H	J	Z	O	V	C	E	T	R	G	B	T	H
U	U	M	Y	B	O	Y	E	D	B	N	U	Q	S	D	N	H	X	A	A
N	V	Y	F	L	L	X	J	A	S	W	S	W	E	Q	A	Q	K	H	T
P	N	W	X	X	G	O	B	O	B	B	Y	Z	P	W	A	I	B	T	B

HOW DID YOU DO? Check your answers on page 64.

45

SCARLET OVERKILL

WORK FOR ME AND ALL YOUR DREAMS WILL COME TRUE!

Scarlet Overkill is the world's first female super villain.

By the time she was thirteen, Scarlet had built her own criminal empire. She is proof to young and old everywhere that you can commit any crime, as long as you believe in yourself.

- **She is impeccably stylish.**
- **Scarlet is quick-tempered, hotheaded, and unpredictable.**
- **She masterminds incredible heists and has a passion for rubies.**
- **Scarlet admits that she is obsessed with the royals and hopes to be crowned queen of England herself one day.**

Scarlet travels from heist to heist in the Scarlet Jet.

Help the queen of crime choose a license plate that would suit her personality perfectly.

HIOFFCR

WLDRIDE

BYE OFFCR

GUILTY

YOLO BBY

MADSKLZ

CYA BYE

L8R CHMP

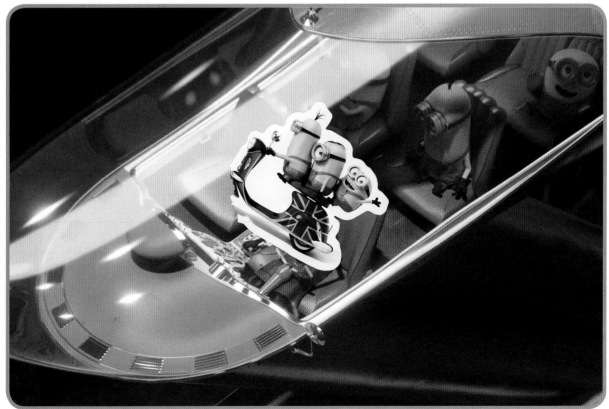

HERB OVERKILL

Herb Overkill is an extraordinary inventor of crazy 1960s villain technology.

His gadgets and machines have many functions, and he can easily reprogram anything. Oh, and he's married to Scarlet Overkill.

THAT IS A GROOVY IDEA!

- **Herb dresses in sharp suits and thin ties.**
- **His inventions include the marvelous Hypno-Hat, Lava-Lamp Gun, and Stretch Suit.**
- **Herb is a bit of a softie and writes Scarlet love letters.**
- **No matter how much evil he does, there's nothing that Herb likes more than seeing a massive explosion.**

Every mad scientist needs a lab, and Herb is no different.

Use this space to design Herb the grooviest lab of the 60s criminal scene. Remember to add a crazy energy source, levers, and places to display his cool creations.

BORED SILLY IN A CAVE

Minions . . . millions of Minions. Let's start counting—it's always best to start at the beginning, at one.

Circle all the flags in the picture and count them. **There are _____ flags.**

Draw an *X* on all the one-eyed Minions and count them.
  There are _____ one-eyed Minions.

Draw a dot on all the two-eyed Minions and count them.
  There are _____ two-eyed Minions.

ARE THERE MORE ONE-EYED MINIONS, TWO-EYED MINIONS, OR RED FLAGS?

HOW DID YOU DO?
Check your answers on page 64.

ICE THE DIFFERENCE

Can you spot ten differences between the two pictures below?

JOKE:
What's an ig?
A snow house without a loo!

WHEN YOU FIND ALL THE DIFFERENCES, STICK KEVIN HERE!

MINION MUDDLE

Being part of a tribe means it's very easy to get tangled up! Just look at this Minion muddle!

Carefully count how many Minions you see in all this mess.

THERE ARE THREE VILLAINS HIDING IN THE PICTURE, TOO. Who are they?

HOW DID YOU DO? Check your answers on page 64.

Criminal
CROSSWORD

Villains, villains everywhere! So many we were able to make a criminal crossword puzzle!

Just decide who is shown in each of the pictures and write their names in the crossword grid below.

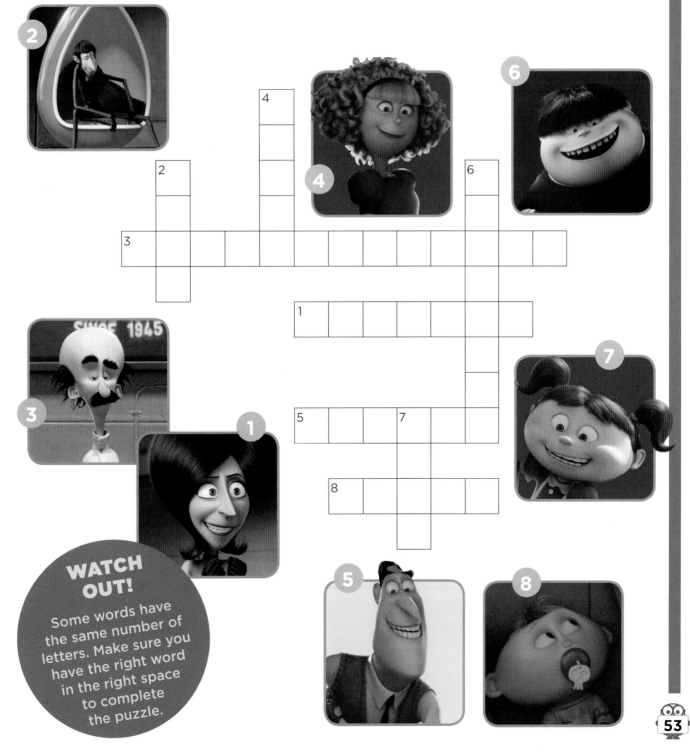

WATCH OUT!

Some words have the same number of letters. Make sure you have the right word in the right space to complete the puzzle.

IT'S TIME FOR YOUR
CLOSE-UP!

Can you recognize which character is which from their close-ups? Find the correct sticker to match each close-up.

1

2

3

4

5

UNSCRAMBLE THE
LETTERS BELOW
TO REVEAL A
CHARACTER'S NAME.

RAELTSC LLIRVEOK

....

MASTERS' HALL OF FAME

The one thing the Minions have learned is that it's easy to find a master . . .

but it isn't so easy to keep one! Take a stroll down memory lane in the masters' hall of fame. Can you match the Minions' uniforms to the master they wore it for?

OH NO, ONE MINION IS MISSING! FIND THE STICKER AND ADD HIM TO THE PAGE.

HOW DID YOU DO?
Check your answers on page 64.

MINIONS THROUGH TIME

Minions have been serving different masters for a VERY long time. In fact, it's been so long that sometimes it's good to sit down and have a recap.

Help these Minions find where they belong in history by adding stickers along the timeline.

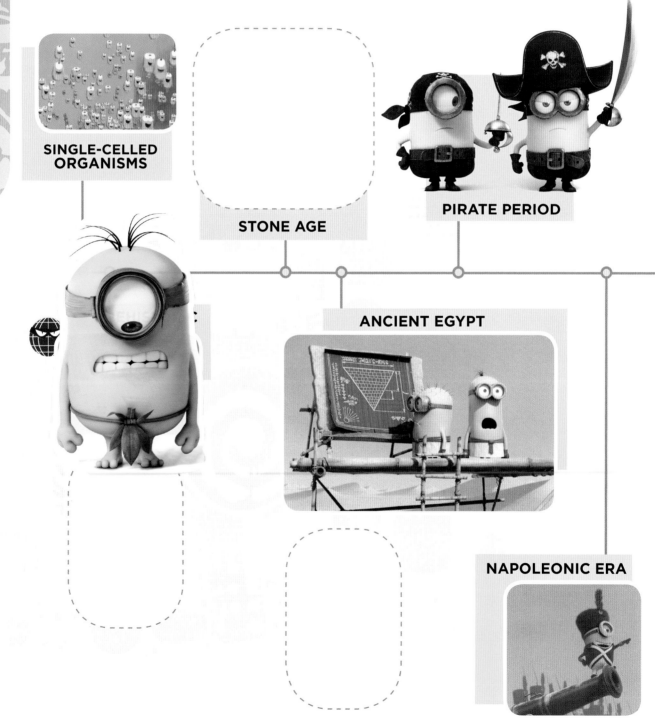

SINGLE-CELLED ORGANISMS

STONE AGE

PIRATE PERIOD

ANCIENT EGYPT

NAPOLEONIC ERA

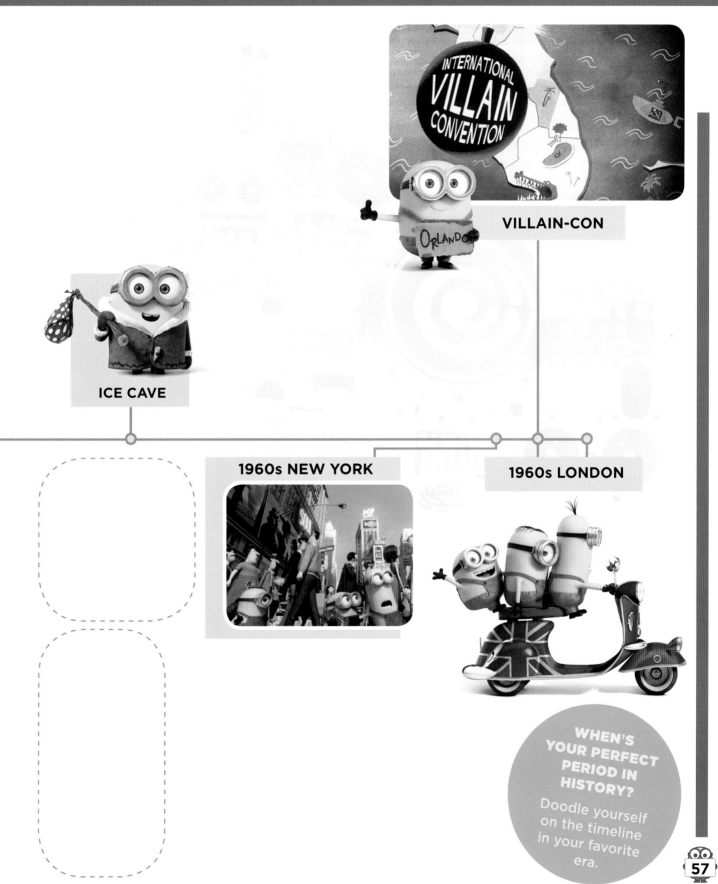

VILLAIN-CON

ICE CAVE

1960s NEW YORK

1960s LONDON

WHEN'S YOUR PERFECT PERIOD IN HISTORY?

Doodle yourself on the timeline in your favorite era.

CODE BREAKER

Brush up on your code-breaking skills to impress your new boss!

USE THE DECODER TO READ THIS SECRET MESSAGE.

UXQNVWJ   BIWNFCVV

_ _ _ _ _ _ _   _ _ _ _ _ _ _ _

CU   VBBFCGE   SBN

_ _   _ _ _ _ _ _ _   _ _ _

GWK   DWGXDTWG!

_ _ _   _ _ _ _ _ _ _ _!

A	B	C	D	E	F	G	H	I	J	K	L	M	N	O	P	Q	R	S	T	U	V	W	X	Y	Z
B	O	I	H	G	K	N	Q	V	T	W	Y	U	R	X	Z	A	J	F	M	S	L	E	C	P	D

HOW DID YOU DO? Check your answer on page 64.

WHO AM I?

How well do you know the Minions?

Using your stickers, can you match the Minions to their shadows?

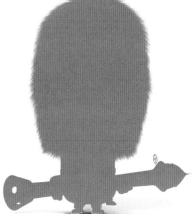

BE MORE MINION

Now's your chance to prove how Minion you really are!

Create your very own Minion profile by writing something about yourself. Use stickers to make it personal.

DESCRIPTION

SPECIAL GADGET OF CHOICE

MY MINION NAME

Hello
my name is

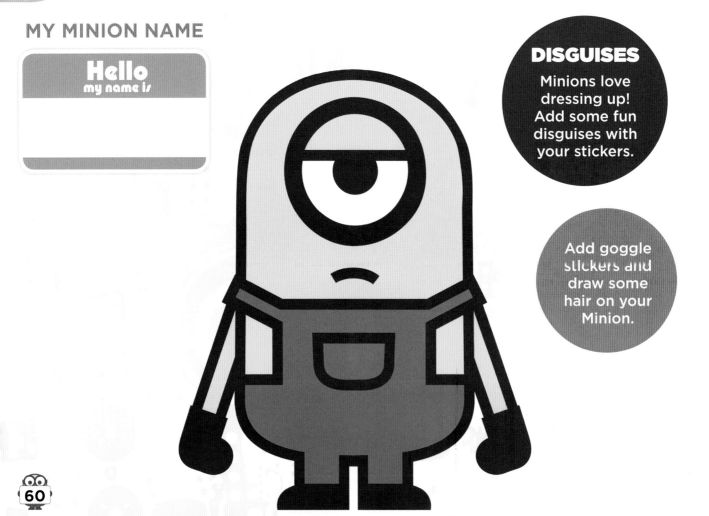

DISGUISES

Minions love dressing up! Add some fun disguises with your stickers.

Add goggle stickers and draw some hair on your Minion.

YOU'RE SO YELLOW!

Congratulations! You helped Kevin, Stuart, and Bob with the greatest challenge for the Minion tribe—ever!

They're out of the cave and ready to get back on the despicable scene looking for a new master. You can help a master crack safes, peek through keyholes, and spot the pitfalls of any period in history.

Using your Minion profile on page 60, draw yourself with Kevin, Stuart, and Bob— because now you're one of the gang!

KEVIN   **STUART**   **ME**   **BOB**

IT'S TIME FOR ANSWERS

PAGE 5

3

PAGE 7

50

PAGE 11

```
J X X H L X P O I U Y T E R E
D V S J K A D X P I U Y X R Q
R O A R J G F S N O I N I M Q
R L X V M U Y R Y U R D F G A
X C C B N F R O T R O R E S S
P A V C U S O A X K A F G H D
O N B X F G A R O A R A O R F
C X D E D F G H H Q C S X A G
I X D E D F G H H Q C S X A G
S P R E H I S T O R I C J S H
S X O T L H S R H O L R A O R
A F A H K X F E J A E R O N J
R D R B J B L X W R R T Y I J
U D X V C V I P P H G R T D K
J S X S S O B G I B X X X X L
```

PAGE 14

PAGE 15

1. C; 2. A; 3. B

PAGE 17

PAGE 18

Build me a pyramid! The largest building Egypt has ever seen!

PAGES 20 & 21

1. cat; 2. five; 3. square; 4. stone;
5. the leader of Egypt;
6. the Nile; 7. hieroglyphics; 8. A

PAGE 22

PAGE 25

PAGE 27

PAGE 28

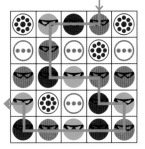

PAGE 30

3	4	5	2	1	6
2	6	1	5	4	3
1	2	6	3	5	4
5	3	4	1	6	2
6	1	2	4	3	5
4	5	3	6	2	1

PAGE 31

pirates
aye matey
ship
ahoy
shark
treasure
plunder
plank

PAGES 36 & 37

1. False. It means "tyrant lizard."
2. False. It was 70 million years ago!
3. True **4.** True **5.** True **6.** True
7. False. It means "son of the dragon."
8. True **9.** True **10.** True
11. False. It was Little Commander.
12. False. He was the ruler of France.

PAGE 38

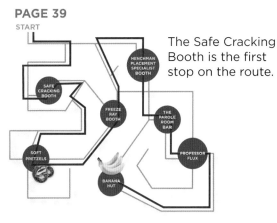

PAGE 39

The Safe Cracking Booth is the first stop on the route.

PAGES 40 & 41

1. Henchmen Placement Specialist Booth
2. Freeze Ray Booth
3. It is next to the Parole Room Bar.
4. Safe Cracking Booth
5. Scarlet Overkill

PAGE 42

ANSWERS

DID YOU FIND A BANANA OR THE VILLAIN-CON LOGO HIDDEN ON EVERY PAGE?

PAGE 44
1. five
2. five (including poster)
3. Around 7:25
4. 1969
5. Banana yellow, of course!
6. Bob

PAGE 45
FAR OUT is hidden 4 times in the grid.

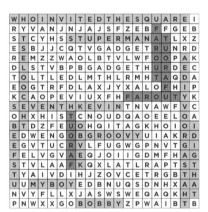

PAGE 50

PAGE 51

PAGE 52
17 Minions
Scarlet, Napoleon, and T. rex

PAGE 53

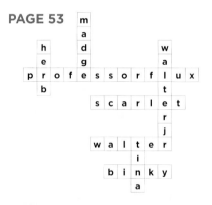

PAGE 54
1. Kevin; 2. Stuart; 3. Bob;
4. Scarlet Overkill; 5. Herb Overkill

Scarlet Overkill

PAGE 55
1. a; 2. c; 3. e; 4. d; 5. b

PAGE 58
Scarlet Overkill is looking for new henchmen!

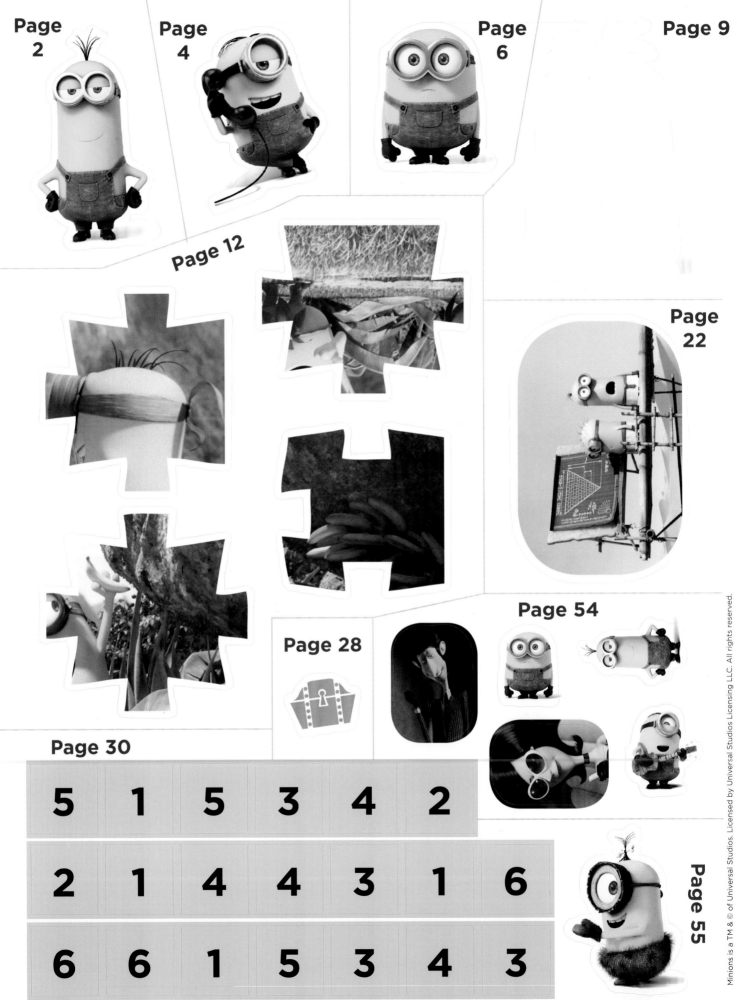

Minions is a TM & © of Universal Studios. Licensed by Universal Studios Licensing LLC. All rights reserved.

Page 46

THAT IS
A GROOVY
IDEA!

Page 17

Page 25

Page 60

Page 45

CRIME ISN'T
PRETTY . . .
IT'S RED
HOT!

Page 47

YOLO BBY   MADSKLZ   HIOFFCR   WLDRIDE

CYA BYE   L8R CHMP   BYE OFFCR   GUILTY

Minions is a TM & © of Universal Studios. Licensed by Universal Studios Licensing LLC. All rights reserved.

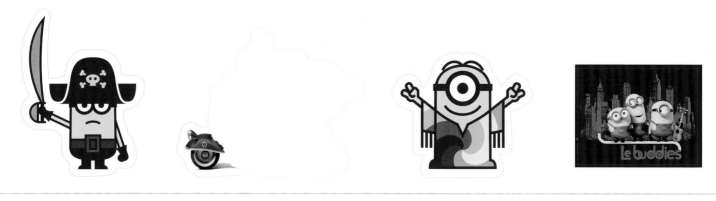

Pages 56 & 57

Minions is a TM & © of Universal Studios. Licensed by Universal Studios Licensing LLC. All rights reserved.

Page 59

Minions is a TM & © of Universal Studios. Licensed by Universal Studios Licensing LLC. All rights reserved.

Minions is a TM & © of Universal Studios. Licensed by Universal Studios Licensing LLC. All rights reserved.

Minions is a TM & © of Universal Studios. Licensed by Universal Studios Licensing LLC. All rights reserved.

Minions is a TM & © of Universal Studios. Licensed by Universal Studios Licensing LLC. All rights reserved.

Minions is a TM & © of Universal Studios. Licensed by Universal Studios Licensing LLC. All rights reserved.

Minions is a TM & © of Universal Studios. Licensed by Universal Studios Licensing LLC. All rights reserved.

Minions is a TM & © of Universal Studios. Licensed by Universal Studios Licensing LLC. All rights reserved.

Minions is a TM & © of Universal Studios. Licensed by Universal Studios Licensing LLC. All rights reserved.

Minions is a TM & © of Universal Studios. Licensed by Universal Studios Licensing LLC. All rights reserved.

Minions is a TM & © of Universal Studios. Licensed by Universal Studios Licensing LLC. All rights reserved.

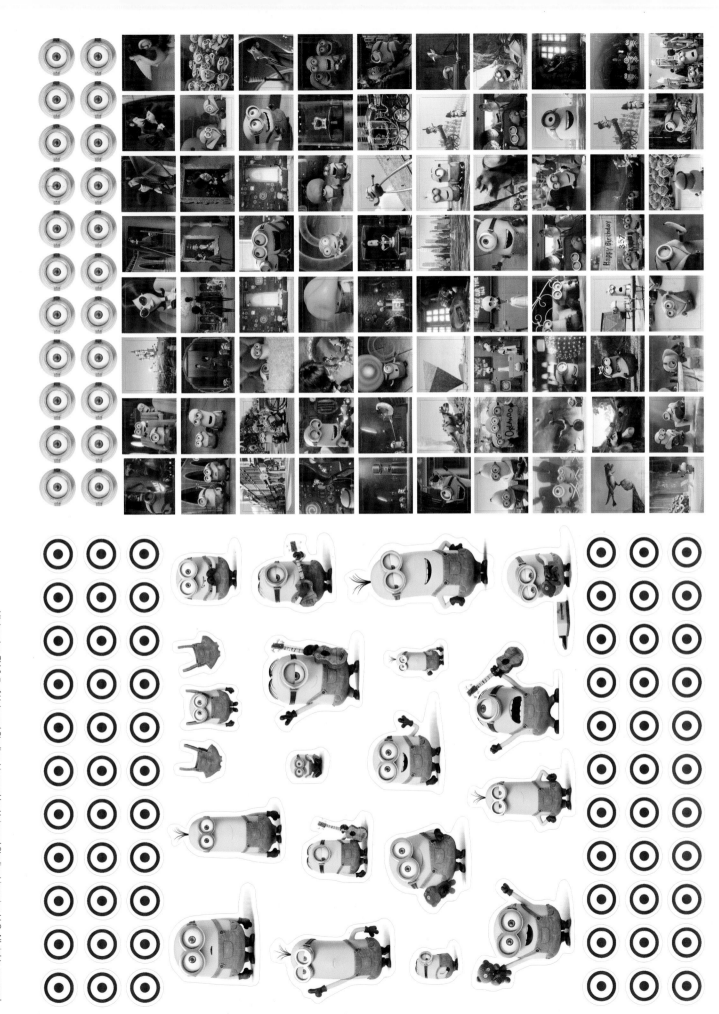

Minions is a TM & © of Universal Studios. Licensed by Universal Studios Licensing LLC. All rights reserved.

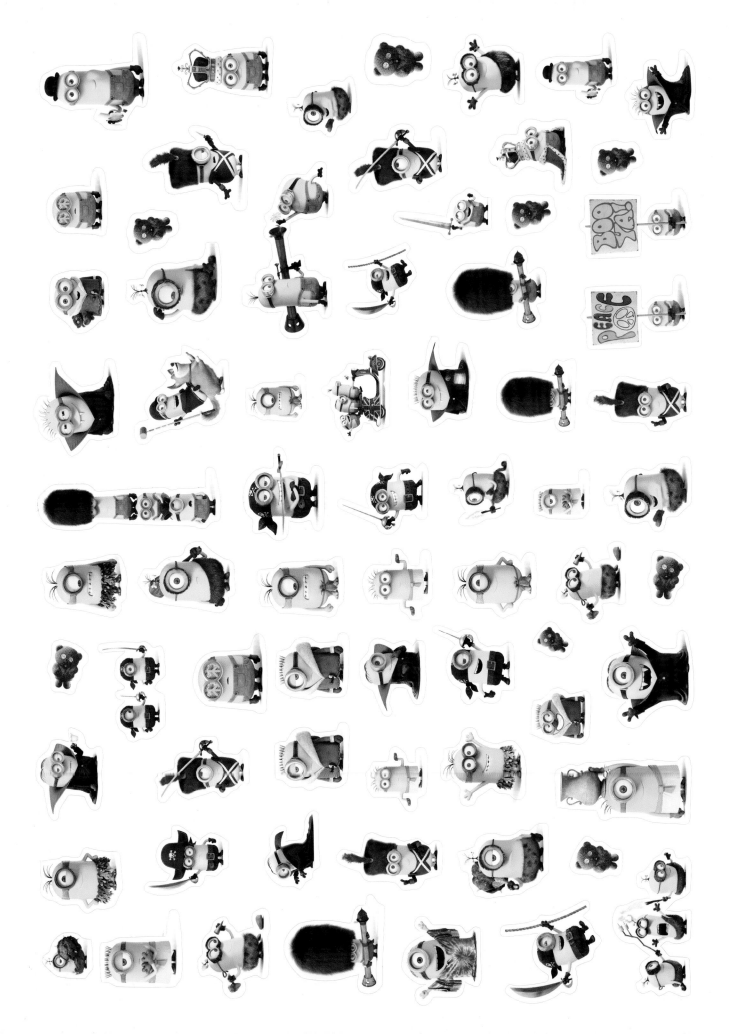

Minions is a TM & © of Universal Studios. Licensed by Universal Studios Licensing LLC. All rights reserved.